Anna Wilson lives in a village in Northamptonshire with her husband, her two children and two black cats called Ink and Jet. She has written two picture books and plans many more books in the

Nina
Fairy Ballerina series.

Nicola Slater lives in the north of England with Dave the cat. Her work can be seen on books and tablecloths around the globe.

Look out for the other books in the

series

New Girl

Best Friends

Show Time

Compiled by Anna Wilson

Princess Stories

Fairy Stories

Nina
Fairy Ballerina

Daisy Shoes

Anna Wilson

Illustrated by Nicola Slater

MACMILLAN CHILDREN'S BOOKS

First published 2006 by Macmillan Children's Books
a division of Macmillan Publishers Limited
20 New Wharf Road, London N1 9RR
Basingstoke and Oxford
www.panmacmillan.com

Associated companies throughout the world

ISBN-13: 978-0-330-43986-2
ISBN-10: 0-330-43986-3

3 5 7 9 8 6 4 2

A CIP catalogue record for this book is available from
the British Library.

Typeset by Nigel Hazle
Printed and bound in Great Britain by Mackays of Chatham plc, Kent

For Lucy and Thomas –
with love and thanks for all your help

Chapter One

"Hurry up, Nina, we're going to be late!" Peri shouted over her shoulder as she flew out the door, still pulling on one ballet shoe.

"If our room wasn't such a tip, I would be ready by now," Nina muttered.

"Fusspot!" Peri teased. "A quick flick of the wand will fix this lot."

"Peri, don't – remember the rules!" Nina was about to remind Peri of the Number One Fairy Academy Rule, which stated that ballerinas should never use their magic in school.

But Peri was too quick. She swished her wand and sang out:

Fairy magic, do your best –
Come and clean away this mess!

At once the room sprang into life, shoes flying into neat rows under the window seat and leotards and tutus fluttering on to hangers and into the wardrobe.

"There," Peri said with satisfaction.

Nina grudgingly admitted the room did look better.

Nina Dewdrop and Periwinkle Moonshine had been at the Royal Academy of Fairy Ballet for a few weeks. They had quickly settled into a routine of assembly, ballet classes, playtime and meals together. Although Nina did get fed up with Peri's untidy habits, the two fairies were the best of friends and they loved sharing a room. In fact, everything about the Academy was perfect as far as Nina was concerned – well, almost everything. If only horrid Angelica Nightshade hadn't been chosen as her mentor.

Nina sped down the corridors of the Academy, away from her room on Charlock corridor and down to the Refectory for breakfast. She could just see Peri in front and was about to call out to

her friend when a silver wand appeared
from nowhere, hovering in mid air. Nina
didn't have time to stop or swerve out of
the way . . .

"Aaaah!" Nina tripped, did a double
somersault and landed on her bottom.
Her carefully combed hair was now
sticking out in all directions, her wings
were crumpled and one of her ballet
shoes had flown off down the corridor.

Peri had heard Nina's scream and,
scooping up the missing ballet shoe, she
flew back to her friend.

"D-did you see what happened?" Nina asked shakily.

"Yes." Peri nodded. "It was that toad Angelica Nightshade. Angelica Nightmare, more like. Why can't she leave us alone? I'm going to get her back for this right now—"

"Just leave it, Peri," Nina interrupted. "I'm not going to let her ruin our day. Quick, let's go and eat. We're already late for class."

After a speedy breakfast, Peri and Nina headed off to the first years' ballet studio. Their other fairy friends were already warming up at the barre, practising their pliés, stretching and preening themselves in front of the mirror. Each fairy was dressed in the Academy's regulation turquoise leotard, tutu and crossover cardigan. They also wore pink tights and turquoise leg warmers and soft ballet shoes. Their wings were crisp and neat,

and each had her hair tied back into a tight little bun. Nina and Peri looked rather messy in comparison.

"Really, fairies, you look as if you've been dragged through a thistle backwards!" scolded their teacher, Miss Tremula.

It was true: Peri's pretty spiky red hair looked a bit like a bird's nest at the best of times, and she always seemed to have ladders in her tights. Today was no exception. Nina, however, took great pride in her appearance and was usually neat and tidy.

"I will not accept scruffiness or lateness, fairies," said Miss Tremula sternly. "Now, come in and warm up."

Nina and Peri worked quickly through some stretches and pliés. Then Miss Tremula told the class what they would be working on that day.

"I want to concentrate on curtseys, fairies," she explained. "You are all a bit wobbly at the knees. You will have to pay special attention to controlling your movements, as a curtsey is one of the most important things a ballerina has to learn. How else will you receive your applause after your first show?" Miss Tremula smiled. "Now, class, watch carefully – I will demonstrate."

The class fell silent and watched as Miss Tremula cast her walking stick aside and flew to the barre. Everyone was always

astounded
by the graceful
way in which the
teacher could fly and
dance in spite of her
incredible age. (Rumour had it
that Miss Tremula was approaching her
one hundredth birthday.)

Miss Tremula stood with her back to
the barre and faced the class. She nodded
to Mrs Wisteria at the piano and, as the
music began, the tiny fairy-ballet teacher
suddenly seemed to grow taller. Slowly

and gracefully she held out the edges of her lilac tutu. Next, with her toes beautifully pointed, she bent her right knee and moved her right leg behind her left. Finally she bent both legs in the daintiest curtsey Nina had ever seen.

The fairies burst into a spontaneous round of applause.

"No wonder she danced for the Fairy Queen!" whispered Peri excitedly.

"Let's see you try now, fairies," Miss Tremula called.

The class immediately fell into line at the barre and held out their tutus, just as their teacher had done.

Soon the whole class was producing a passable curtsey. Mrs Wisteria kept the fairy ballerinas in time as she played a waltz on the piano, and Miss Tremula hobbled up and down the room, leaning on her stick and making encouraging noises as her pupils practised.

Suddenly the concentration was

broken by a loud knock on the studio door. A small, skinny fairy with jet-black hair bounded into the room and announced that she had a message from the headmistress.

"Oh no," Nina groaned. The fairy was Tansy Mugwort, one of Angelica's sidekicks.

"Go ahead, Tansy. Give the class the message," Miss Tremula said impatiently. She did not like her lessons to be interrupted.

"Madame Dupré has just received the dates for this term's examinations," Tansy said, smiling smugly. "They have been brought forward this year."

There was a buzz of conversation in the studio as the first years wondered what this would mean.

Tansy then handed Miss Tremula a piece of pink paper, trimmed with gold. At the top of the page was the gold crest of the Royal Board of Ballet Examiners.

"Oh dear,"
Miss Tremula
sighed as she read
the letter. "I'm afraid
it's true, class. The
exam is in two
weeks! We've
got even less
time than I
thought to
prepare. Well, thank you,
Tansy. You can go now.
In fact, class is over
anyway, so go and
have a break, fairies. I
need to rethink my lesson plans."

With that, Miss Tremula hobbled off.
And the fairies left the studio feeling very
subdued and rather worried.

Chapter Two

"We don't even know yet what we are supposed to be learning for the exam," Nina said to Peri. "We won't stand a chance of passing."

"Nina, you're such a worrier!" Peri said kindly, putting her arm around her friend. "You'll be fine. You won the scholarship, don't forget. *And* you're already one of the best ballerinas in the class. I can't even find matching leg warmers in the morning, let alone perform a plié without falling over."

To take their minds off the exam,

Nina and Peri went to see if they'd got
any post.

Miss Meadowsweet, who worked in
the office, was sorting the morning's
letters and parcels into the correct pigeon-
holes when Nina and Peri walked in.

"Good morning, fairies!" she trilled.

"Good morning, Miss Meadowsweet,"
the fairies replied in unison.

"I'm glad you're here,
Nina," Miss
Meadowsweet
said, smiling. "A
special letter has
just arrived for you by
grasshopper express!"
She handed the
envelope to Nina.

Nina squealed
when she caught
sight of the large
loopy writing on the
envelope. "It's from

Heather Pimpernel, my fairy godmother!" Nina ripped the envelope open and pulled out a sheet of lavender-scented paper. More of the loopy writing covered the page. "She wants to come and visit, Peri! Oh, this is so exciting. Heather is such fun."

"Cool! Can I meet her?" Peri asked. "I haven't got a fairy godmother. How come she sent her letter by express?" she added.

"It says here that she's coming in two weeks! She probably didn't trust hummingbird-mail to deliver the letter in time. I bet she's heard about the ballet exam being brought forward. She knows so many people on the examiners' board. She used to be an examiner herself. Maybe she'll be able to give us some tips, Peri."

"That would be great," Peri agreed. "We're going to need all the help we can get."

The next day was a Saturday and Nina was going to Hornbeamster, a big town where there was a cinema and lots of shops.

"Will you come with me?" she asked Peri. "I'm meeting up with Poppy and I know she's dying to see you again."

"I'd love to!" Peri said. "Poppy always livens things up," she added, thinking back to the magic Nina's sister had performed in the fairies' room on the first day of term.

"Yes," Nina said doubtfully. "Well, let's hope she's a bit calmer this time."

"There you go again, Little Miss Worry," Peri teased. "Come on, let's get shopping!"

In no time at all the fairies arrived in Hornbeamster. Nina suggested that they go to Bushel & Broomley, the shoe shop, before meeting Poppy.

"Sounds great," Peri said.

Nina had a secret reason for wanting to go to Bushel & Broomley. The last time she had been there, she had seen the most beautiful dainty silk ballet shoes with ribbons made from daisy chains. She had set her heart on them, but her mother had said they were not practical. Ever since that day, Nina had not stopped dreaming of owning a pair of daisy ballet shoes, and today she wanted to show them to Peri.

Peri could not believe her eyes when the two fairies walked into Bushel & Broomley.

She rushed over to the ballet section
and started riffling through all kinds of
pink, lilac and pastel blue shoes. In no
time at all, she had picked out a pair of
pale blue silk ballet shoes with blocks. She
pulled them on and tried
walking around on points.

"Argh! This is
agony! I don't think
I'll ever be able to
deal with blocks," she
groaned. Nina hastily
grabbed her friend's
arm. "Peri! Stop
clowning around!"
she hissed. "Come
here. I want to
show you a
special pair
of ballet
shoes."

Nina led Peri to the shelf
where she had seen the daisy ballet shoes.

But to her horror there was only one pair left! Nina hurriedly tried them on, and luckily they were a perfect fit.

"What am I going to do? If they sell out, I'll probably *never* be able to find such a beautiful pair of ballet shoes again!" Nina cried.

Peri agreed that the daisy ballet shoes were the prettiest she'd ever seen. "You'll have to work on your mum to let you have them, Nina," she said. "They'd make perfect performance shoes."

"That's just what I said," Nina explained, "but Mum wouldn't listen. Oh, I *can't* miss out on the last pair!"

The two fairies reluctantly left Bushel & Broomley and went to meet Poppy under the town's dandelion clock.

Nina's little sister was already there, her wings fluttering with impatience.

"Nina! Peri! At last! Mum's gone to do some shopping. I'll meet her back here later. Hey – I'm starving! Let's go to

Sprinkles and you can tell me all your news."

Sprinkles was the best cafe in Hornbeamster and served the most delicious marshmallow hot chocolate in the whole of fairyland. It came in tall glasses and had melting marshmallows floating in it and mountains of mouth-watering fluffy cream. And of course it had chocolate sprinkles on the top.

"Let's have fairy cakes too," Poppy said, licking her lips greedily.

Soon all three fairies were giggling and chatting away between slurps of hot chocolate. Nina told Poppy about Angelica's friend Tansy Mugwort, and Peri made the others laugh with a very good impression of Angelica bossing Tansy around.

Suddenly Nina started looking nervously over her shoulder. "Peri, stop. Look over there. I don't believe it – it's Angelica!"

Sure enough, the mean mentor had just walked into Sprinkles with Tansy.

"Well, well. If it isn't eensy-weensy Nina and her ickle fwends," Angelica said, tossing her blonde hair. "I wouldn't eat all that cake if I were you, Neeny. You'll be too heavy to fly and you'll fail your exam. Now wouldn't that be a shame?"

"Yeah, Nina," Tansy broke in. "Can't have the scholarship fairy getting fat on fairy cakes, can we?"

Poppy was furious. How dare Angelica talk to her sister like that? She narrowed her eyes at the two older fairies and flicked her wand under the table . . .

"What in the name of all enchantment – ARGH!" Angelica shrieked. She and Tansy found themselves covered from top to toe in pink icing. Angelica's long hair was sticking to her face, and her wings had hardened under all the sugar. "You little pipsqueak!" she growled at Nina. "How DARE you? You'll regret this, you mark my words!"

"But it wasn't—" Nina tried to explain, but Poppy grabbed her hand, beckoned to Peri, and the three fairies flew to the door.

"What did you do that for?" Nina shouted at Poppy.

"She only got what she deserved," Poppy said defiantly. "It's about time Angelica saw what we Dewdrops are made of!"

Chapter Three

Nina, Peri and Poppy met Mrs Dewdrop under the dandelion clock. Nina had promised Poppy that she would keep quiet about what had happened in Sprinkles, but couldn't help mentioning the ballet shoes.

"Oh, Mum, I saw those daisy ballet shoes again in—"

"Nina," Mrs Dewdrop broke in, impatiently, "I *said* you couldn't have them." Nina tried to protest, but Mrs Dewdrop held up her hand. "I spent a fortune on all your ballet clothes on our last shopping trip. And what about that ballet bag I sent you last week? You can't have everything—"

"But, Mum!" Nina butted in. "There's only one pair left!"

Mrs Dewdrop softened as she saw the look of desperation on her daughter's face. "Listen, maybe if you manage to get top marks in your exam . . . I might just *think* of buying them for you. Oh, goodness, look at the time," she added. "Come on, Poppy. We'll have to fly right away if we're going to catch our dragonfly."

Nina felt a lot happier after extracting this promise from her mother. Now all she had to do was concentrate on getting top marks.

The rest of the weekend passed peacefully, with no more trouble from Angelica or Tansy, and Nina had almost forgotten about the incident in Sprinkles.

After breakfast on Monday, Miss Tremula greeted the fairies with her usual warm smile and explained what they would be learning for the exam.

"You will all be expected to curtsey beautifully at the beginning and end of the exam," she said, "and obviously the examiners will want to see all five ballet positions."

The first years nodded. This didn't sound too bad.

Miss Tremula continued. "The most challenging part of the exam is the 'original dance' section. Mrs Wisteria will play a piece of music from the ballet *Sleeping Beauty*, and you must invent a dance. It will be from the scene at the end when Aurora wakes up after her hundred years asleep. I would not advise you to attempt anything too challenging," Miss Tremula cautioned. "As you know, we haven't got much time to prepare."

Class was soon under way and once everyone was warmed up Miss Tremula asked the fairy ballerinas to gather round. "I'd like to take you through a few moves that you could put into your own dances," she explained. "Now, let me show you how you will be expected to pirouette . . ."

Miss Tremula carefully placed her

stick on a chair and drew herself up to
her full fairy height. She bent her right
leg so that her foot was touching her left
knee. Then she gracefully went up on to
the tip of her left toe. Holding her arms
down gently in front of her, she spun
round in a perfect circle. The fairies all
cheered as Miss Tremula curtseyed.

"You needn't be so
surprised!" Miss Tremula
laughed. "I may be
an old fairy, but I
still know a thing or
two."

The class laughed
along with their teacher.
Then, in pairs, the fairy
ballerinas practised their
pirouettes. Some tried
to cheat by fluttering
their wings to make
them spin more quickly, but
Miss Tremula immediately

spotted such sneaky tricks.

"Come now, fairies. The Royal Board of Ballet Examiners won't let you get away with *that* sort of nonsense. You'll be failed straight away. And no one from my class has ever failed their first exam."

Once the class had perfected the pirouette, Miss Tremula decided that the fairies were ready to think about their original dances. The class sat down again and listened as Mrs Wisteria struck up the first few chords of the last scene in *Sleeping Beauty*.

Nina was determined to do her best. She had been practising a particularly

challenging move called a "grand jeté".
This meant leaping up and doing the
splits in the air. It was very difficult – the
main problem Nina had was landing
gracefully afterwards. But she was
absolutely determined to include this
move in her dance.

It will be just right for the end of
Sleeping Beauty, Nina thought to herself. If
I manage to leap gracefully, it will show
how happy Aurora is to be woken by the
handsome prince.

After a couple of false starts, Nina
managed a
wonderful jeté
and landed
softly
without a
sound in fifth
position.

Peri ran up to her friend and threw her arms around her. "No wonder you won the scholarship, Nina. You're the best!"

"That was spectacular, Nina," Miss Tremula agreed. "Can you please show the whole class?"

Nina blushed and was just getting ready to do another jeté when Tansy Mugwort burst into the studio, slamming the door behind her. Peri caught a glimpse of Angelica lurking in the shadows out in the corridor.

"Tansy! This is most irregular!" Miss Tremula exclaimed. "We are in the middle of a class."

"I know, I'm sorry, miss," Tansy said, out of breath from flying, "but it's an emergency. Miss Meadowsweet needs to see you and Mrs Wisteria in the office."

"Oh, really? Well, I suppose we'd better go immediately, Mrs Wisteria. Could you please continue with your

demonstration, Nina,"
Miss Tremula said.
"And stay with
my class while
I'm gone, please,
Tansy. I'm sure I
won't be long."

Once Miss
Tremula and Mrs
Wisteria had left
the studio,
Tansy turned
to close the door
and shot a nasty smile
in Nina's direction as
Angelica slipped into
the room.

"Right then,
scholarship slug."
Angelica smirked, folding her arms and
looking straight at Nina. "Let's see what
you're made of."

Chapter Four

"**D**on't listen to her, Nina," Peri advised.

"That's right," agreed Nina's friend Nyssa. "We all think you're fantastic. Why don't you show Angelica that jeté you just did?"

"No," Nina said in a small voice.

"Of course she won't," Tansy sneered. "She doesn't even know what a jeté is!"

"You mean *you* don't," Peri muttered.

"Stop it, Peri," Nina said nervously. "I don't mind. I'll do it."

The class stood back as Nina

prepared to do the grand jeté again. She took a deep breath and looked at her friends, who smiled encouragingly. Nina took a run and leaped through the air. She soared, her toes pointed beautifully, her arms spread wide in a graceful arc. Nina seemed to fly, yet her wings were not moving. Then there was a bright flash of light and Nina suddenly plummeted down on to the hard floor.

She lay clutching her right leg as tears coursed down her cheeks.

"*That's* what comes of showing off," Angelica said with a sigh. "I'll go and find Miss Tremula. You stay here, Tansy." And she flew from the room, with her nose in the air.

Nina's friends crowded round her.

"What happened, Nina? Are you all right?" Nyssa asked.

"Of course she's not all right!" Peri snapped.

"Stop it, please," Nina whispered. "I think I've broken something."

"Don't worry," Peri said soothingly. "Doctor Leaf will know what to do."

At that moment Miss Tremula hurried into the studio.

"Oh, Nina, dear!" she cried. "How in all fairyland did this happen? You were doing *so* well when I left. I don't know what Tansy was talking about anyway. Miss Meadowsweet didn't think there was

any emergency in the office." She sighed.
"There's certainly an emergency *here*
though. Let's get you to the doctor."

Miss Tremula waved her wand and
sang out:

> *On my count:*
> *One, two, three,*
> *Carry Nina*
> *To the surgery.*

At once, four little fairies in nurses'
uniforms appeared from nowhere, each
holding one corner of a stretcher. They
put it down on the floor and gently

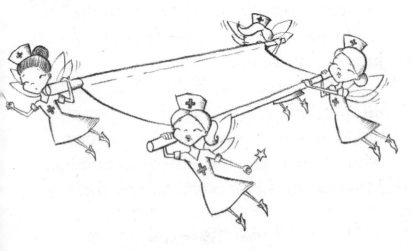

placed Nina on to it. Then they lifted the stretcher into the air and flew out of the room.

"I'll go with her!" Peri cried.

Miss Tremula nodded. "The rest of you can have a break," she said softly. "I think you've all had a bit of a shock."

Nina was soon lying on a fresh white bed in the Sickbay. Doctor Leaf, the Academy's fairy doctor, rushed over straight away.

"Hmm. Nasty," she said, examining Nina's leg. "This is not a simple fracture. I'll try a few spells and we'll see what we can do."

Doctor Leaf tried all manner of rhymes and ointments, but none of the usual magic medicine seemed to have any effect.

"This is most peculiar," the doctor said. "I have seen many ballet accidents in my time, but very few have refused to react to my medicine before. I think someone must have cast a spell on you. And, in this case, it looks like only the person who cast the spell can undo the magic. Do you have any idea who might be behind this?"

"I think I know!" said Peri.

"No!" Nina whispered sharply. She managed to lean over the side of the bed and poke Peri in the arm.

"OK, OK," Peri muttered under her breath. Then she turned to the doctor. "I don't have proof – but I've got a fair idea who did this. And I intend to find out if I'm right," she said firmly.

"Well, let me know as soon as you are sure," said Doctor Leaf seriously. "In the meantime I will give you something for the pain, Nina." And she handed Nina a glass of silver-birch tonic.

Nina grimaced as she swallowed the bitter liquid.

"Right," said Doctor Leaf. "I'll leave

you in peace now – and so should you,
Periwinkle. Try to get some sleep, Nina."

As soon as the doctor had gone, Peri
hissed at Nina, "Why didn't you tell her
about Angelica?"

Nina was starting to feel comfortably
drowsy and didn't want an argument.

"Peri, stop it. If Angelica knows I've
told on her, she'll try something worse.
Besides, we don't know for sure that it
was her fault."

"Who else could it have been?" Peri

shouted. "And anyway, what could be worse than being laid up in the Sickbay with a broken leg two weeks before the ballet exam?"

But all Peri received in reply was a loud snore from her fairy friend.

Chapter Five

Peri and Nyssa had decided to pick some flowers for Nina to cheer her up. Nyssa also thought that spending some time outside would help her friend calm down. Peri was still furious about Nina's fall.

"I just need to go to the loo first," Peri said. "Will you wait for me?" She fluttered down the corridor to the bathroom. She had just gone into a cubicle and shut the door when she heard voices outside.

"Ha ha ha!" someone laughed. "Did

you see the look on that slug's face when she fell?"

Angelica! Peri thought. She stayed as still as she could and prayed that Angelica wouldn't notice that one of the cubicles was occupied.

"Yeah!" said Tansy. "And her little squirt of a friend – Cherry Moonwhatsit."

"Peri – yeah, I've never seen *her* speechless before! I really wiped the grin off those irritating little pixie features," said Angelica gleefully.

Ha! thought Peri. So she *did* do it!

"It's so cool that you are the only one who can remove the spell," Tansy crowed. "You're so clever, Ange."

"Yes, I know, and *don't* call me Ange!" Angelica hissed. "Luckily for me, old Doc Leaf is rather past her prime these days. Nettle stings are about all she's good for. She'll never find the cure for this little problem! I found it in an old book in the Advanced Magic section of the library."

Peri was boiling with fury. I must think of a plan, she told herself.

At that moment Nyssa came into the bathroom and Angelica and Tansy left, giggling to each other.

"Peri?" Nyssa called out. "Are you all right? What were those two up to?"

Peri opened the door and came out looking very subdued. "I don't know," she muttered. It was better to keep her discovery to herself until she had a plan.

Nina spent the day in the Sickbay, writing a long letter to her mother and Poppy, telling them everything that had happened and how miserable she was.

At least one good thing might come out of all this, she thought. Mum might take pity on me and buy me those daisy ballet shoes.

Nina was finding it hard to rest. Her leg was held up in a sling and was swathed in cobweb bandages to keep it still. It soon became very uncomfortable. She was relieved when Doctor Leaf said she could start to have visitors.

Miss Tremula came to visit Nina at the end of the day and promised to send the letter by grasshopper express. "Your mother will get it quickly then, dear," she said. "Now, I thought you might like to listen to some music, so I'll lend you my Daisy Discplayer and some of my discs. I've put *Sleeping Beauty* in there so that you can think through some moves for the exam."

Nina looked as though she was going to cry.

"Now now, dear," said Miss Tremula, putting her hand on Nina's arm. "I told you none of my class has ever failed an exam before, didn't I? And I don't expect *you* to be the first. Make sure you sleep well – rest is very important when you are injured. I'll come and see you again tomorrow."

The next day Nina received a string of visitors. Peri arrived straight after breakfast with a huge bunch of bluebells.

"Peri! They're gorgeous!" Nina exclaimed. "Thanks."

"I picked them yesterday with Nyssa," Peri said, leaning over the bed to give her friend a careful hug. Then she caught sight of the Daisy Discplayer. "Wow!" she cried, examining the machine closely. "This is the latest model! Look at this – you can even record on to discs." She showed Nina one of the buttons on the machine. "In fact, that gives me an idea," Peri said quietly to herself.

"What's that?" Nina asked.

"Oh, just a thought," Peri said hurriedly. "Listen, I haven't got much time before class, so let me show you some moves I've been working on for the exam."

Peri immediately started clowning around, and made Nina laugh by performing pliés and pirouettes while flying upside down and cartwheeling around the room.

"Ouch! Stop!" Nina cried out. "You're making me laugh too much! Aurora would *never* be able to do all that after sleeping for a hundred years!"

"What in fairyland is going on?" Doctor Leaf came rushing in, but smiled when she saw the cause of all the hilarity. "I think it's time you went to class, Periwinkle. Nina mustn't get too overexcited."

Peri flew down next to Nina. "Sorry, Doc. See you later, Nina," she added, giving her friend a quick kiss. She was about to leave when the discplayer caught her eye again. "Er, Nina . . ." she said shyly, "could I borrow this for a bit?"

"Well, I should probably ask Miss Tremula first," said Nina uncertainly.

"Don't worry — I'll tell her I've got it. My old thing's broken you see, and I need to listen to *Sleeping Beauty* again this evening."

"All right," Nina agreed. But she couldn't help feeling a little uneasy. What was Peri up to?

Chapter Six

Nina was visited every day by well-wishers from her class and members of staff. Everyone brought presents: bunches of wildflowers, packets of nuts and seeds, fairy cakes and even a packet of golden honey-drop sweets.

Peri was the most regular visitor. She also made Nina laugh the most, with her amusing accounts of what had gone on that day in class.

"You'll never guess what Nyssa managed to do today!" she told Nina one evening towards the end of the week.

"She pirouetted
so hard, her tutu flew
off!"

Nina giggled.

"Even Miss Tremula was
in fits," Peri continued. "She had to wave
her wand and command the tutu to
come back!"

"Oh, poor Nyssa," Nina said.

"Oh no, she was laughing too," said
Peri hastily. She noticed that Nina had
gone very quiet. "Look – try and forget
about the accident. I'm working on a

plan – don't you worry. You'll be back in class next week, I promise."

"But that only leaves a few days before the exam!" Nina said, tears pricking her eyes. "And I'll never get those shoes . . ."

Peri jumped up, her emerald-green eyes glittering like fireworks.

"Oh, I forgot to say – I'm meeting your mum and Poppy in Hornbeamster tomorrow," she said, grinning. "And then they're coming back with me to visit you."

"Oh, Peri! Do you think you could persuade her to take a trip to Bushel and Broomley?" Nina cried, suddenly perking up.

"That's *exactly* what I intend to do," Peri said, with a cheeky grin.

Peri woke up early on Saturday morning. She couldn't wait to see Mrs Dewdrop and Poppy. But she also had a little bit of shopping of her own to do.

First, she whizzed to a music shop and bought some new ballet discs for Nina to listen to.

I know she will love *Giselle*, Peri thought to herself as she sifted through the discs on display. As she went to pay, Peri caught sight of some blank discs by the till. "Are these for the new Daisy Discplayer model?" she asked the fairy shop assistant.

"That's right."

"So I could record me and my friends singing?" Peri asked excitedly.

"Yes, of course!" The shop assistant smiled at the spiky-haired imp jumping up and down in front of her. "Are you planning a nice surprise for someone?" she asked.

"Something like that!" Peri said with a wink.

Mrs Dewdrop and Poppy were already waiting outside Bushel & Broomley when Peri arrived. Poppy was unusually quiet and, for once, didn't seem at all excited to see Peri. Mrs Dewdrop didn't look all that happy either.

"What's the matter, Mrs D? Poppy?" Peri asked anxiously.

Mrs Dewdrop sighed miserably and reached out to give Peri a big hug. "Oh, Peri!" she cried. "We're too late. The last pair of daisy ballet shoes has *gone*!"

It was a mournful trio of fairies that trudged through the gates of the Royal Academy of Fairy Ballet that lunchtime.

"I feel dreadful!" groaned Mrs Dewdrop. "I should have let Nina have those shoes when she first saw them."

"Yeah, you should," said Poppy unhelpfully.

"Shh, Poppy," hissed Peri. "Can't you see how upset your mum is? Listen, take her straight to the Sickbay. I'll be along in a minute. And whatever you do, *don't* tell Nina about the shoes."

"Why? Where are you going, Peri?"
Poppy asked suspiciously. "And what's in
that bag you're carrying?"

"Oh, nothing – nowhere. I mean, I
just need the loo," Peri said hastily. "But
before that," she added, muttering to

herself, "I've got a letter to send – by grasshopper express!"

Nina was delighted to see her mum and sister. They had brought her lots of treats and were full of stories about her friends back in Little Frolic-by-the-Stream. The Dewdrops were chatting away when Peri burst into the Sickbay and slammed the door behind her.

"It was her!" she cried. "I've got proof!" Peri was madly waving a music disc in one hand and carrying Miss Tremula's discplayer in the other.

"What are you talking about, dear?" Mrs Dewdrop asked.

"I've recorded Angelica saying that it was *her* spell that made Nina fall!" Peri said urgently. "Quick, we must play it to Doc Leaf immediately! Angelica is the only one who can undo the spell and make Nina's leg better. Come with me, Poppy!"

Before Mrs Dewdrop or Nina could ask any more questions, Poppy and Peri had disappeared down the corridor.

They were back in seconds with Doctor Leaf.

"It's true, Nina," the doctor said grimly. "I'm afraid that Angelica Nightshade was responsible for your fall."

"I think you'd better tell me what's been going on," said Nina, looking at Peri.

"Yes, I would like an explanation too, please," said Miss Tremula, who had just come into the Sickbay.

"I think there are two more fairies who should hear this," said Doctor Leaf. "I shall just go and fetch them."

Doctor Leaf soon returned with the headmistress, Madame Dupré, and a red-faced Angelica Nightshade.

"What's going on, Peri?" Nina whispered.

"Quiet, please!" commanded Madame Dupré. "Nina, I'm very sorry to have to tell you that we have reason to believe dark fairy magic was to blame for you breaking your leg." Madame Dupré turned to Peri. "Periwinkle, will you please turn the discplayer on for us?"

Peri pressed the Play button on the

Daisy Discplayer. Suddenly Angelica's voice filled the Sickbay.

"It's been great not having that scholarship slug around this week, hasn't it, Tansy?"

"Yeah! No more 'Nina this, Nina that'!" agreed Tansy. *"And it looks like no one's been able to figure out yet who cast the spell — so they don't know who has to undo the magic! Doesn't look like Nina will be taking the exam either. You're so clever, Ange."*

"Don't call me Ange!" Angelica said angrily. *"It is hilarious, though, isn't it? I can't believe I've got away with it!"*

Miss Tremula leaned over and pressed Stop. A stunned silence filled the Sickbay.

"I am afraid, Angelica Nightshade, that you very much *haven't* 'got away with it'," said Madame Dupré sternly.

"Yeah, *Ange!*" Poppy said, grinning cheekily.

Madame Dupré ignored Poppy and

continued: "As you have all just heard, we have conclusive proof – thanks to this recording – that you, Angelica, are responsible for the spell cast on Nina."

Nina caught Peri's eye, and her friend winked. So *that* was what Peri had been up to with the discplayer! Nina thought.

"What have you to say for yourself, Angelica?" said Madame Dupré.

Angelica opened her mouth, but no words came out.

"There is nothing to be said," said Doctor Leaf. "It only remains for you to undo the magic, Angelica. And I hope you realize what a dangerous and naughty thing you have done."

To everyone's surprise, Angelica was crying, tears rolling down her face and soaking her leotard.

"I-I'm s-sorry!" she squeaked. "I really am. I just couldn't bear all the attention Nina was getting. I'll undo the spell right away."

"You certainly will!" said Miss Tremula angrily. "And then you can fly off and pack your bags. You are no longer welcome at the Academy."

"Ahem, Miss Tremula," said Madame Dupré gently. "That is a matter for *me* to decide, don't you think? I don't believe in making hasty decisions."

Angelica glanced gratefully at the headmistress.

"However," the headmistress continued, "I don't think we can let this go unpunished, Angelica. You will be responsible for cleaning the bathrooms for the rest of the year — with*out* the help of any magic!"

Angelica nodded glumly and went over to Nina's bed.

"I *am* sorry, Nina," Angelica said quietly. "I promise I'll leave you alone from now on. You're a great ballerina and you deserve the scholarship." Then she whispered a string of words and waved her wand over Nina's injured leg. There was a shimmer of silver light, and the bandages fell away.

"Look! I can move my leg again!" Nina cried in delight. She struggled out of bed and stood up. "It really is better! Oh, thank you, Peri! And thank *you*, Angelica!" Nina beamed, her wings fluttering happily.

Everyone cheered and applauded as

Nina curtseyed, and even Angelica managed a smile.

"I'll be able to do my exam now, won't I, Miss Tremula?" said Nina, smiling. "Looks like you might have to buy me those shoes after all, Mum!"

Mrs Dewdrop and Poppy exchanged nervous glances.

Chapter Seven

The next week passed in a flurry of extra classes for the First-Year ballerinas. At last the day of the exam came, and Nina anxiously waited her turn outside the Grand Hall. She joined a long queue of first years, all dressed neatly in pink leotards especially for the exam.

Peri had been examined first and came out of the hall looking relieved.

"How did it go?" Nina asked.

"OK, I think," Peri replied. "Thanks to your help, I got through the exercises.

It's the *Sleeping Beauty* dance that's the worst bit."

"Well, it's thanks to *you* that I'm here at all," said Nina, hugging her friend. "I still can't believe that you managed to outwit Angelica. Oh well, my turn now. Wish me luck!"

Nina opened the door to the hall. Inside, four fairy examiners were sitting behind a long desk. She recognized one of them as Magnolia Valentine – the famous prima ballerina who had first inspired Nina to become a fairy ballerina!

"Good morning, Nina," said Magnolia kindly. "Let's see what you've learned so far at the Academy, shall we?"

Nina went through all five ballet

positions perfectly. She pointed her toes
beautifully and did some truly amazing
arabesques. But then it was time for the
Sleeping Beauty dance – and Nina had her
only shaky moment. She tried to do the
grand jeté, but lost her footing at the last
minute. The memory of the fall in class
was still too strong, and Nina found that
she couldn't manage the leap. She left the
hall hanging her
head and was
very quiet for
the rest of the
morning.

Peri tried her best to distract her friend over lunch, but Nina was convinced she had failed. She was just telling Peri for the tenth time how she had slipped up on the grand jeté, when she was interrupted by Miss Meadowsweet.

"Nina! There you are! I've got a lovely surprise for you," Miss Meadowsweet said, smiling. "After all that's happened, I bet you'd forgotten you were expecting a visitor this week, hadn't you?"

A plump, elderly fairy flew into the Refectory behind Miss Meadowsweet. She was wearing a floor-length golden gown, and her silvery hair was held into a bun with a tiara that glistened with moonstones.

"Hello, Nina dear!" she trilled.

"Heather!" Nina gasped, and ran to hug her fairy godmother. "Peri, this is Heather Pimpernel – remember I told you about her?"

Peri grinned at the older fairy. "You've arrived just in time, Heather," she said. "Nina needs cheering up."

Just then Miss Tremula came into the Refectory too, leaning on her cane.

"You should have something else to smile about in a minute, Nina," said her teacher. "It's time for the exam results. All first years to the Grand Hall, please!"

There was a flurry of wings as the first years jostled their way into the

Grand Hall. One by one their names and their results were called by Magnolia Valentine. Every fairy had passed the exam and was awarded a medal and a certificate.

Peri was over the moon. "I can't believe it!" she whispered as she flew back to Nina.

At last it was Nina's turn.

"Ah! Nina Dewdrop, the scholarship fairy," said Ms Valentine. "The first part of your exam was excellent. You show magnificent potential." Nina looked relieved. "But," Ms Valentine continued, "I'm afraid that we couldn't give you the top mark of distinction." Nina looked downcast. She had so wanted to get top marks. "Your original dance needs a little more work, as I think you realize. However, we *have* awarded you a merit. You deserve recognition for the fact that you took the exam at all, after what happened to your leg." The examiner

smiled and gave Nina
her medal and
certificate.

Nina turned to face her friends, who
were all clapping enthusiastically.

"And *I* have something for you too,
Nina," added Heather Pimpernel. "A
little pixie sent me a note to tell me that
you had set your heart on a particular

pair of ballet shoes. Unfortunately, Bushel
and Broomley weren't able to help me,
but by calling in a few favours I
managed to get you these." Heather
handed Nina a silvery packet tied up
with honeysuckle ribbons.

Nina took the parcel
from her fairy
godmother and
carefully
unwrapped it.
She gasped.
Inside were her
dream ballet shoes
with the ribbons made
from daisy chains.

Nina leaped up into
the air and waved
her wand high
above her
head in
delight. An
arc of shimmering

stars shot out of her wand and settled on the assembled group.

"The daisy ballet shoes! Oh thank you, Fairy Godmother!" Nina cried, throwing her arms around her. "And thank you, 'little pixie'," she added, rushing to hug Peri. "What would I do without you?"

Collect three tokens and get this gorgeous Nina Fairy Ballerina ballet bag!

There's a token at the back of each Nina Fairy Ballerina book - collect three tokens, and you can get your very own, totally **FREE** Nina Fairy Ballerina ballet bag.

Send your three tokens, along with your name, address and parent/guardian's signature
(you must get your parent/guardian's permission to take part in this offer)
to: Nina Fairy Ballerina Ballet Bag Offer, Marketing Department, Macmillan Children's Books, 20 New Wharf Road, London N1 9RR

Nina Fairy Ballerina Bag Offer

1 Token

Collect 3 tokens and get your free ballet bag!
Valid until 31/12/06

A selected list of titles available from Macmillan Children's Books

The prices shown below are correct at the time of going to press.
However, Macmillan Publishers reserves the right to show new retail prices
on covers, which may differ from those previously advertised.

Anna Wilson

NINA FAIRY BALLERINA

New Girl	ISBN-13: 978-0-330-43985-5	£3.99
	ISBN-10: 0-330-43985-3	
Best Friends	ISBN-13: 978-0-330-43987-9	£3.99
	ISBN-10: 0-330-43987-1	
Show Time	ISBN-10: 978-0-330-43988-6	£3.99
	ISBN-13: 0-330-43988-X	

Poppy Shire

MAGIC PONY CAROUSEL

Sparkle	ISBN-13: 978-0-330-44041-7	£3.99
	ISBN-10: 0-330-44041-1	
Brightheart	ISBN-13: 978-0-330-44042-4	£3.99
	ISBN-10: 0-330-44042-X	

All Pan Macmillan titles can be ordered from our website,
www.panmacmillan.com, or from your local bookshop
and are also available by post from:

Bookpost, PO Box 29, Douglas, Isle of Man IM99 1BQ
Credit cards accepted. For details:
Telephone: 01624 677237
Fax: 01624 670923
Email: bookshop@enterprise.net
www.bookpost.co.uk

Free postage and packing in the United Kingdom